Excalibat

Story by David English   Pictures by Jan Brychta

Foreword by Brian Johnston   Introduction by Dr W.G. Grass

ARTHUR BARKER

AN IMPRINT OF GEORGE WEIDENFELD AND NICOLSON LIMITED LONDON

Published in Great Britain by
George Weidenfeld & Nicolson Limited
91 Clapham High Street London SW4 7TA

ISBN 0 213 16949 5

Printed in Italy

Foreword by Brian Johnston

The other day as I was munching some chocolate cake, two baby bunnies were playing on the lawn. They looked so happy and quite unconcious of any possible dangers. As I threw them a piece of cake, I thought what a pity it was that they had no bunny bat and ball with which to play cricket.

It used to be an insult to be called a Bunny at cricket. It meant that you always made zero and dropped every catch. But now the Bunbury Cricket Club have changed all that. All Bunnies like myself are proud to be members and to share in the amazing exploits of Ian Buntham – this time as he hits Ivan the Terribull for six with the magic bat, Excalibat.

Brian Johnston

Introduction

I was sitting with dear Florence Nightingale just the other night. I stared into her lamp and asked her of ages past. She told me of Buntham the Unready, a mightly champion of the people who had wielded his bat against many a foe. And what of the future?

We drew closer to the lamp. At that moment, there was revealed Goldenhare Gower, Viv Radish, Allan Ram and a cricket team called the Bunburys. Extraordinary, I thought. But there again, hadn't Gordon won at Kartoon?

So now let the mysterious tale of Excalibat unfurl.

Dr W.G. Grass
Forest of Dean, 1876

'It's still raining and the clouds are getting darker,' moaned Ian Buntham, staring blankly out of the window.

Bunbury had been playing the foxes from Flowery Field in a local league match and getting the brush-off. Now as the rain formed a sheet of water across the pitch the players mooched around the dressing room. Some read the newspaper, others idly watched television.

'Turn it over, Viv,' said Edbuns. *'Top of the Hops* is on the other side.'

Rodney Munch and Dennis Lettuce played cards. 'I'll raise you two bucks and see you, Denno,' chirped Munch confidently.

Little Rajbun wandered around the room staring up at the bats hanging up on the oak-pannelled walls.

'Where do all those old bats come from?' Rajbun asked Old Holbun.

The kindly manager explained why each bat was famous.

'Jack Hopps hit 316 with this one against Whiskertown in 1924 . . . This one was Herbert Hutchcliffe's first bat, and Dr W.G. Grass scored over 3,000 runs with this faithful blade . . .'

At the end of the line Rajbun peered up at an empty case.

'And what about this one?' enquired Raj.

'Ah! Now . . . There's a tale my friend. This case belongs to the most famous bat of all . . . Excalibat.'

The name 'Excalibat' stirred the players from their pastimes.

'Let me tell you the story,' smiled the manager, settling into his favourite chair.

In the year 300 BB (Before Buntham) King Arthur Barker and the beautiful Queen Bunnivere ruled over this land from the enchanted Castle of Bunelot.

King Arthur had many good knights. There was Sir Laughalot, Allan the Lamb, the Duke of Head-in-Burrow, Goldenhare Gawain and the Green Knight. They were popular with the people, who worked happily in the carrot and lettuce fields for their rulers.

Then one day Bunburye was invaded by Ivan the Terribull and his Bunbarians. They were cruel and greedy and terrorized the kingdom.

'King Arthur, the wrath of Terribull is upon you!' bellowed the bull, breathing fire and scorching the crops.

The bunnies tried to defend their land, but they were terribully outnumbered and finally retreated to the sanctuary of the castle.

'Everyone inside!' ordered the King. 'Up with the drawbridge.'

For days Ivan the Terribull and his army laid siege to the castle.
King Arthur and his knights fought bravely as they struggled to keep
their attackers at bay.

King Arthur called his trusty knights to the council chamber.

'Sire,' said Sir Laughalot, 'surely Olde Holbun the Magician could find some
means to help us?'

'Mmm. A good idea,' mused the King, fiddling with his beard. 'Bring him to me.'

Olde Holbun was brought to the King and the two of them huddled together
in whispered conversation.

Many hours passed before the Magician summoned the King to the room where he cast his spells and made his magic. The Magician revealed to the astonished King a golden bat fixed in a great stone. Alongside was an empty wooden casket with the name 'Excalibat' upon it.

The beleaguered bunnies were awestruck at this miraculous sight.

'Find me the rabbit who can lift Excalibat. I need a bunny in a billion!' boomed the King.

One by one the nobles tried to lift the bat out of the stone but none of them was able to.

In a barn somewhere inside the castle walls, Buntham the Unready was enjoying his afternoon nap. Suddenly the door burst open, stirring Buntham from his slumber. Bleary-eyed from a thousand lost nights, he saw before him Katherine his wife, and his three children.

'Wake up, father,' shouted his young son Liam the Little.
'You must go to King Arthur.'

King Arthur and his Knights were in despair. Outside the walls of the castle, Ivan the Terribull and his hordes were storming the ramparts yet again.

'Still I can find no one,' sighed the King, sadly shaking his head.
'But wait, who is this?'

'He says he's called Buntham the Unready, my Liege,' announced Sir Laughalot.

'Very well, there is the bat,' said the King. 'You try.'

'What, this one?' said Buntham, lifting it easily out of the stone.

There was a hush as the amazed assembly watched Buntham twirling Excalibat
from one paw to the other.

'To the battlements, Buntham,' shouted the King triumphantly.
'Let's hope we're not too late.'

High on the ramparts, Buntham wielded Excalibat, boldly repelling the Bunbarians'
every attack. 'Look how he hitteth them for six!' cried the bunnies.

'O long-haired one!' bellowed Ivan the Terribull. 'I challenge you to one final tournament to prove who is the strongest!'

'Only too happy to oblige,' retorted Buntham, for once in his life ready for anything.

All was prepared for the joust.

Wearily the citizens of Bunburye took their places in the grandstand.

'Let battle commence,' cried Buntham, astride his faithful charger Red Bun.

Crash went Excalibat against the top of Ivan the Terribull's helmet. But Ivan was terribully strong. He swung round knocking Buntham off his horse.

The anxious onlookers gasped, 'Buntham, Buntham, look out!'

As Ivan the Terribull charged, Buntham held Excalibat aloft.

'Come on trusty bat. Don't fail me now,' muttered Buntham through clenched teeth.

The reflection of the sun on Excalibat momentarily dazzled Ivan. The mighty bull staggered back.

That was all Buntham needed. Quick as a flash he pounced, bringing Excalibat down on the snout of the raging bull.

Standing above the conquered beast, Buntham decreed: 'Never darken this land again.' And the bull turned tail and slunk off into the forest.

Seeing their leader defeated, the Bunbarians fled and were never
to be seen again.

Buntham waved Excalibat aloft and was cheered by the happy throng.

'Buntham! Buntham!' chanted the joyful bunnies in the castle.

'Buntham! Buntham! . . .'

Back in the pavilion, the players were so engrossed in Old Holbun's story that they didn't hear umpire Dickie Purred calling.

'Buntham, is it still raining?'

'What? Oh, yes! I think so,' said Ian, gazing absent-mindedly out of the window.

'What happened to Excalibat?' asked Rajbun.

'It disappeared, Raj,' said Old Holbun, 'and has never been seen since that day.'

At that moment the sky darkened and a shaft of light shone down on to the water-logged pitch.

'I think you all better come over here,' said Ian Buntham in a trembling voice. 'There's something you ought to see . . . Excalibat is back!'